with an afterword by

Paul Binder

Founder and Artistic Director of
The Big Apple Circus

Look, everyone! It's a parade!

1

The circus is coming! The circus is coming!

Hurry! Let's follow the clown. . . .

I hope there will be elephants.

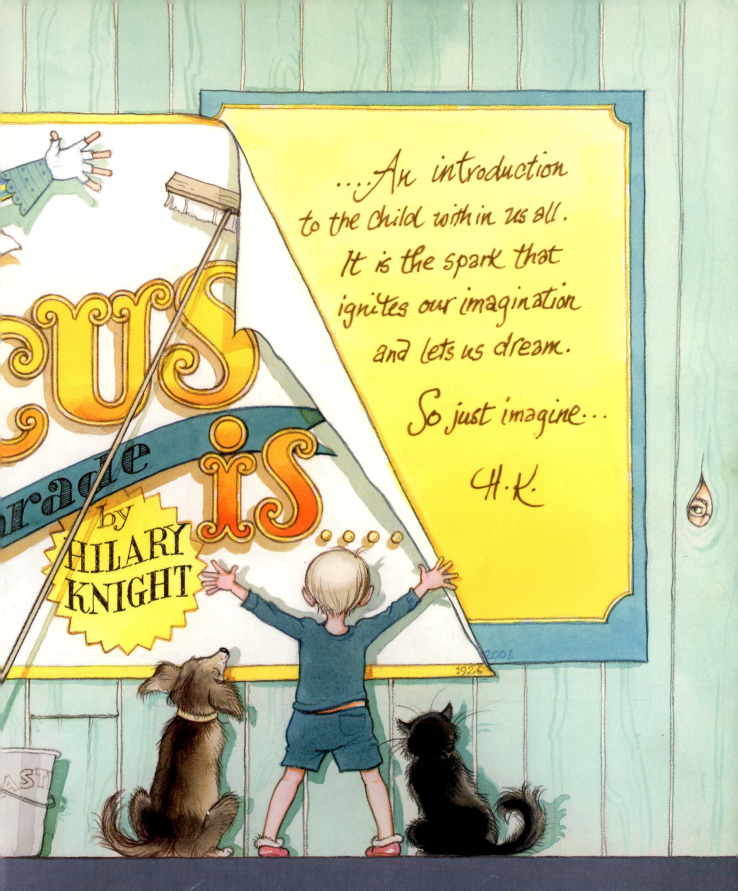

...An introduction to the child within us all. It is the spark that ignites our imagination and lets us dream.

So just imagine...

H.K.

by HILARY KNIGHT

PARADE

TODAY!

COME ONE COME ALL

A GOLDEN BOOK • NEW YORK

www.goldenbooks.com   www.randomhouse.com/kids
Library of Congress Control Number: 78-068425
ISBN: 978-0-375-84066-1 (trade)—978-0-375-94066-8 (lib. bdg.)
PRINTED IN CHINA   10 9 8 7 6 5 4 3 2 1

Listen! Can you hear music?

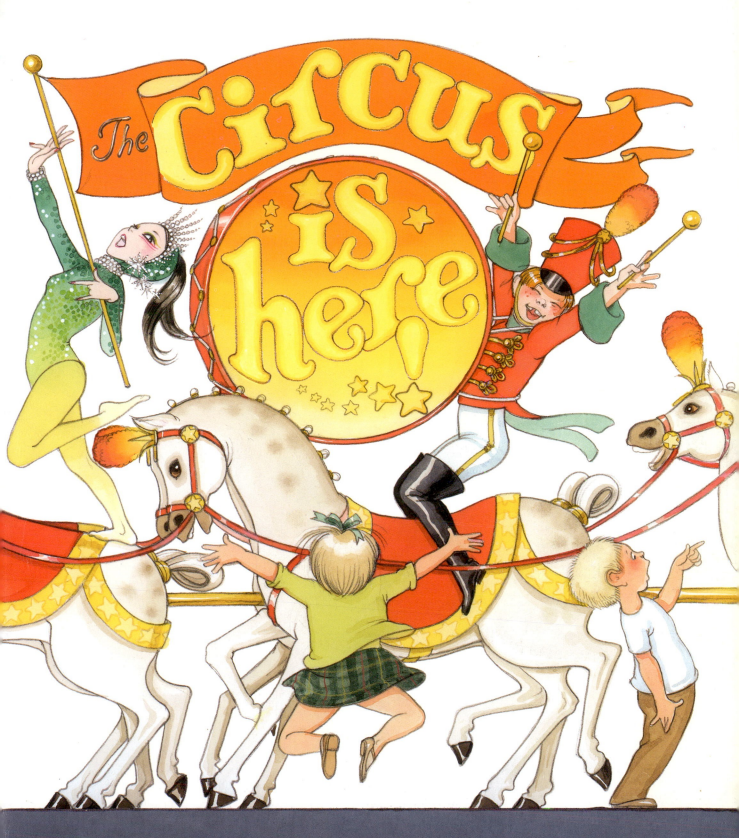

Oh, WOW! Look what's coming!

Crash! Boom! Brass blast!

'And pop goes . . . a button?! Do I hear purring?

Cats and kitties, sweet and snarly!

Where's some catnip?

Clowns by the cabload . . .

how many can you count?

I'm turning upside down

with tambourines, tightropes, and teeterboards.

Up! Up! UP! High-Stepping Steeds!

I want to be a bareback rider.

Oh, Outrageous Orangutans!

But where are the elephants?

From China! A tumbling troupe

that twirls, twists, and turns!

Pirate Pranks and Powder Kegs!

Boom! Let's follow the cannonball clown. . . .

Swish into the safety net.

But where's his other boot?

The wild horsemen of Turkmenistan

on their sturdy stamping stallions.

Canine capers: prancing poodles,

baby bulldogs . . . but no elephants!!!

A fabulous float of fantastic folks.

RENALDO RUBBERMAN

SALOME SERPENTINA

INNIE ATURA & WEE MAC

Each one a wonder!

Summertime in Garden Greenery.

Then a seasonal switch!

Suddenly it's silvery, slippery, and snowy . . .

a winter Polar Paradise!

I adore acrobatic chimpanzees

flying on the high trapeze.

South America! Land of Incan gold,

gauchos, and the untamed Amazon!

Now North America! Here's Buffalo Bill

and his Wild West Show!

A bumper crop of bumbling

basketball buffoons . . . and a giraffe!?!

Elegant, exotic Africa!

And . . . finally . . . Look!

Elephants! Elephants! ELEPHANTS, at last!

Big and small, I love them all!

Oh! What a dazzling spectacle!

Hilary Knight and the Circus

Hilary was born in 1926 in Roslyn, New York. It was there that he and his older brother, Joey, saw their first circus. (In fact, that's them below, running off to see it again.) This book is the result of a lifelong fascination with the circus and all things theatrical. It was inspired by many extraordinary people and events:

• After the Knight family moved to Manhattan in 1932, Hilary's first stage show was *Jumbo*, Rodgers and Hart's circus musical, at the legendary Hippodrome.

• Hilary's artist-writer parents, Clayton Knight and Katharine Sturges, opened up a whole new world to him when the family traveled to South America in 1937.

• Just before entering military service during World War II, Hilary enrolled in the Art Students League of New York. His instructor, Reginald Marsh, taught him not only how to draw, but also how to make the drawings move.

• In the 1940s, costume designer Miles White dressed many famous productions. Hilary's favorite was *The Pirate*. Later, Miles and Hilary became friends. White also designed Ringling Brothers Circus for many years.

• Long interested in the theater, Hilary did poster designs for producer Harry Rigby (the stiltman to the left) and his press agent, Henry Luhrman (depicted as a child in a wagon on page 3).

That was so exciting!

Some people have called me a dreamer. After all, I set out to create something that had never been done before: a permanent performing circus for New York City that would do shows in a tent (!) on the Plaza (!) at Lincoln Center! I suppose that was a pretty big dream.

Well, the truth is I don't dream much, but when I do, I dream big. Big dreams with brilliant flashes of color; powerful men; sensuous women; people of all races, shapes, and sizes; savage and tamed wild animals and ridiculous clowns. Apparently Hilary Knight, the author of *The Circus Is Coming,* dreams big as well. His book is the stuff of dreams, fantasy, and magic: bodies flying through the air . . . people facing wild beasts . . . chimps and orangutans making us feel like we're looking at ourselves in a funhouse mirror . . . beautiful ladies riding camels, leopards, and stallions . . . masked actors wearing big noses and floppy shoes . . . and elephants (at last!) . . . all performing with artful grace and beauty! These are sleep images turned real, the intensely visual and visceral re-creations of happy dreams. And aren't we all dreamers? Isn't that why we're here watching a fantastic circus parade . . . audience and performers alike?

This is an especially rich book for veteran fans of the circus and, of course, for those discovering it for the first time. Just look at page five. Could that be young Hilary himself, already in awe of the parade that's *yet to come*? This wonderful book shows that when we dream, we can anticipate and empower our future.

I think that's why I like going back to it over and over again.

—*Paul Binder*

Don't you just love a parade?

Hilary Knight

is the illustrator of more than fifty books. The circus plays a part in his own *Where's Wallace?*, as well as Kay Thompson's *Eloise in Moscow*. He has a lifelong love for the circus, from humble tent shows to arena spectacles.

In 2006, while on assignment for *Vanity Fair*, Hilary visited the Cirque d'Hiver in Paris for the Festival Mondial du Cirque de Demain, the annual competition for the top circus acts in the world. It was there that he met . . .

Paul Binder

. . . a Brooklyn native who earned a Dartmouth BA and a Columbia MBA before joining the San Francisco Mime Troupe, where he learned to juggle. With juggling partner Michael Christensen, he toured Europe as a street performer, joined Annie Fratellini's Nouveau Cirque de Paris, and returned to America to create a circus with the same artistic excellence and theatrical intimacy he had experienced in Europe. In 1977, Paul founded the Big Apple Circus, and he remains its artistic director and ringmaster to this day.

Come! Let's start all over . . .

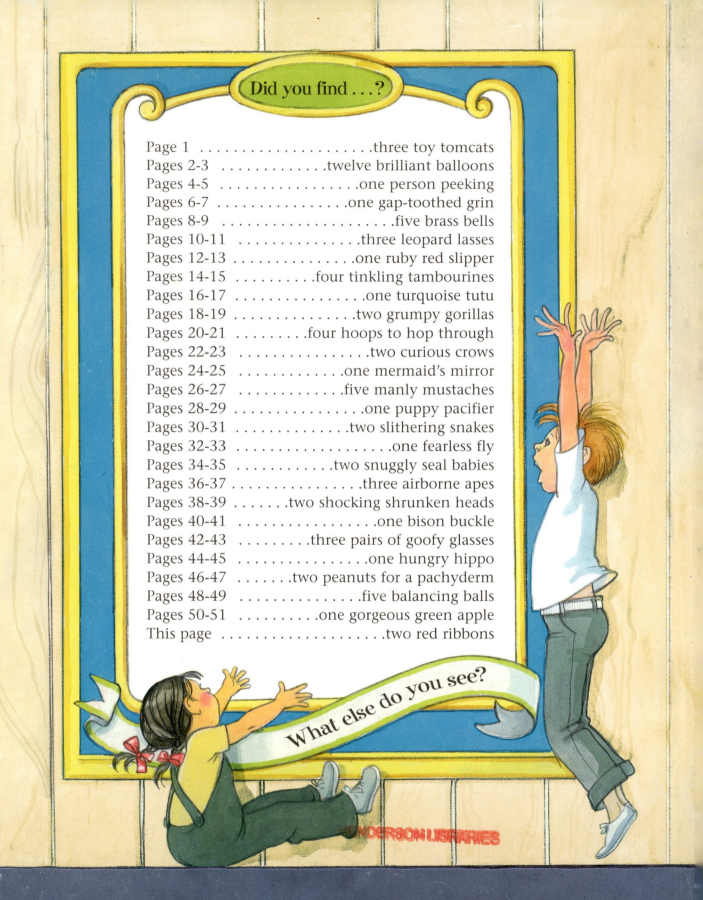

Did you find . . . ?

What else do you see?

. . . there's so much to see!